Grassland Animals

Biome Beasts

Rourke
Educational Media
rourkeeducationalmedia.com

A Division of
Carson
Dellosa
Education®

Lisa Colozza Cocca

BEFORE AND DURING READING ACTIVITIES

Before Reading: *Building Background Knowledge and Vocabulary*

Building background knowledge can help children process new information and build upon what they already know. Before reading a book, it is important to tap into what children already know about the topic. This will help them develop their vocabulary and increase their reading comprehension.

Questions and Activities to Build Background Knowledge:

1. Look at the front cover of the book and read the title. What do you think this book will be about?
2. What do you already know about this topic?
3. Take a book walk and skim the pages. Look at the table of contents, photographs, captions, and bold words. Did these text features give you any information or predictions about what you will read in this book?

Vocabulary: *Vocabulary Is Key to Reading Comprehension*

Use the following directions to prompt a conversation about each word.

- Read the vocabulary words.
- What comes to mind when you see each word?
- What do you think each word means?

Vocabulary Words:
- *abandoned*
- *burrows*
- *decomposers*
- *migrate*
- *nocturnal*
- *nutritious*
- *prey*
- *savannas*
- *steppes*
- *temperate*

During Reading: *Reading for Meaning and Understanding*

To achieve deep comprehension of a book, children are encouraged to use close reading strategies. During reading, it is important to have children stop and make connections. These connections result in deeper analysis and understanding of a book.

 ## Close Reading a Text

During reading, have children stop and talk about the following:

- Any confusing parts
- Any unknown words
- Text to text, text to self, text to world connections
- The main idea in each chapter or heading

Encourage children to use context clues to determine the meaning of any unknown words. These strategies will help children learn to analyze the text more thoroughly as they read.

When you are finished reading this book, turn to the next-to-last page for **Text-Dependent Questions** and an **Extension Activity**.

Table of Contents

Biomes

A biome is a large region of Earth with living things that have adapted to the conditions of that region.

NORTH AMERICA

SOUTH AMERICA

= Grassland Biome

Grassland biomes are open, fairly flat stretches of land covered mainly by grasses. There are two main types of grassland biomes: **temperate** and tropical.

Temperate Grasslands

Temperate grasslands include prairies and **steppes**. Both of these have hot summers and cold winters. Prairies have moderate rainfall. Grasses and flowers grow in the rich soil here, but there are few trees.

prairie in Kansas

Steppes receive only about half as much rain as prairies. The grasses that grow here are shorter than those that grow on prairies because of the dryness.

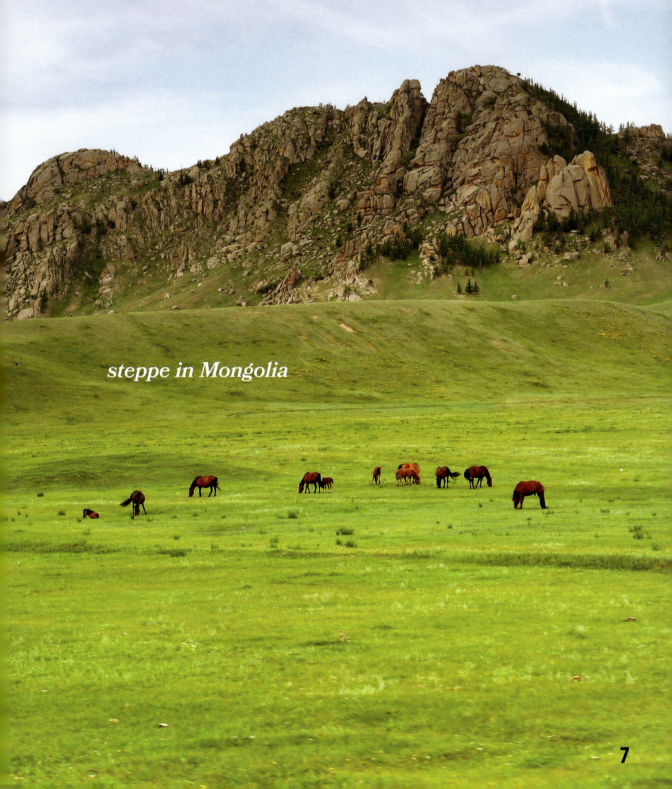

steppe in Mongolia

Open Prairies

Prairies are home to many ruminants. Ruminants are animals with four-part stomachs. They can eat tough grasses and use them for energy. Bison are ruminants. Their broad, flat-topped teeth can chew the tough grasses found here.

Bison can be up to 6.5 feet (1.98 meters) tall at the shoulder. They can weigh more than a ton (0.9 metric ton). Bison have poor eyesight, but excellent hearing and sense of smell. They have few predators because of their size.

Did You Know?

Bison remain active throughout the winter. Their fur grows so thick that snow can land on it and not melt. They use their curved horns to dig through snow to reach the grasses below.

Elk are also ruminants. An elk eats about 20 pounds (9 kilograms) of grasses and herbs each day. Its light, waterproof summer coat helps it stay cool. Its thick, wooly winter coat is about five times warmer than its summer coat. It uses its hooves to clear snow off the grasses to eat in winter.

Did You Know?

Elk will tuck their thin legs under their bodies when they rest to keep them warm.

The prairie chicken likes to eat ants, grasshoppers, and leafhoppers. It will eat seeds and grass if needed, but it will fly as far as 30 miles (48 kilometers) to find the food it likes. This bird builds its nest of grass, twigs, and feathers on the ground. The tall grasses around it keep the nest hidden from predators.

Prairie chickens don't **migrate** in the winter. Feathers on their legs and feet help keep the birds warm in the cold. When snow falls, the chicken stays in its nest under the snow. The snow blocks the wind and helps the bird stay warm.

Much of the activity in prairies takes place underground. Prairie dogs use sharp claws to dig a system of connected tunnels and **burrows**. During the day, they use their sharp teeth to gnaw on plants, roots, and seeds, but most of their time is spent digging or repairing their town.

Did You Know?

The largest known prairie dog town spread over 25,000 square miles (64,750 square kilometers) of land in Texas. It was home to about 400 million prairie dogs.

The prairie dog's work helps many other animals. Jackrabbits, badgers, weasels, burrowing owls, toads, and rattlesnakes move into the burrows.

burrowing owl

The black-footed ferret lives in the burrows. This **nocturnal** animal's excellent sight, hearing, and sense of smell help it hunt in the dark tunnels. This ferret's favorite food is its host. Each ferret eats more than 100 prairie dogs every year.

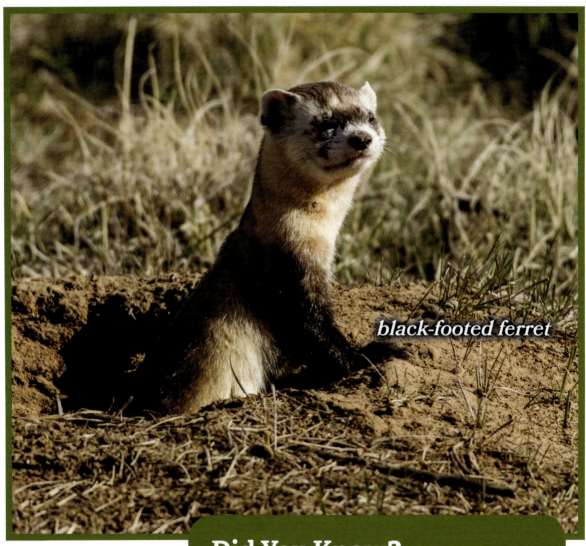

black-footed ferret

Did You Know?

Prairie dogs prepare for winter by storing some extra food in their burrows. They can go for long periods without food or water if they must.

The tiger salamander spends its day in a prairie dog burrow. It has a short snout, sturdy legs, and a long tail. At 14 inches (36 centimeters) long, it is the largest land salamander. It leaves at night to hunt for worms, insects, frogs, and other salamanders to eat.

The markings on a tiger salamander depend on the subspecies to which it belongs. This amphibian is a blotched tiger salamander.

Steppe Grasslands

Animals in steppe grasslands live in drier conditions. Przewalski's (shuh-VAHL-skees) horses need plenty of water. During dry spells, they break the soil with their sharp hooves to find water underground.

Did You Know?

Przewalski's horses adapt their activity to the weather. They are most active during the coolest hours of hot days and the warmest hours of cold days.

Przewalski's horses have short, stocky bodies with big heads. They grow a thick, warm coat in the winter and shed it in the spring.

These plant-eaters live in herds for protection from predators, such as wolves and snow leopards. The horses can hear and smell danger from great distances. If they can't escape, they use their strong teeth and legs for protection.

Argali sheep, the largest sheep in the world, live on steppe grasslands. They have a short, dark coat during summer and a long, lighter coat during winter.

The sheep are plant-eaters. Females feed in higher locations where the food is less **nutritious**, but there are fewer predators. Males feed in lower areas with better food, but more predators.

Did You Know?

Argali sheep live in herds for safety. These long-legged, fast runners move as a herd when predators approach. If one gets separated from the herd, it plays dead, or lies still, until the predator leaves.

black vulture

Black vultures also live in steppe grasslands. These large, long-legged birds have excellent day vision, but no sense of smell. The black vulture follows a turkey vulture, which has an excellent sense of smell, to a food source—a dead animal. Several black vultures land on the food together to force the much bigger turkey vulture away.

Tropical Grasslands

Tropical grasslands, or **savannas**, are warm to hot all year. The rainy season lasts six to eight months. During this time, 20 to 50 inches (50 to 127 centimeters) of rain falls. Grasses grow as high as seven feet (two meters) tall and trees grow scattered across the land. The rainy season is followed by a long dry season.

Many animals thrive in the warm, wet climate of the savanna. Fires are common during dry months. These blazes kill insects and drive away rodents and lizards.

lion in a savanna

Termites support hundreds of other living things in this biome. They are the main **decomposers** in the savanna. Termites build mounds made of spit and their own waste material. The mounds measure 6 to 20 feet (two to six meters) high. The termites live in an underground nest below the mound.

Did You Know?

Termites build tunnels in their mounds that allow air to flow in and out of the nest. It acts like air conditioning during the hot months.

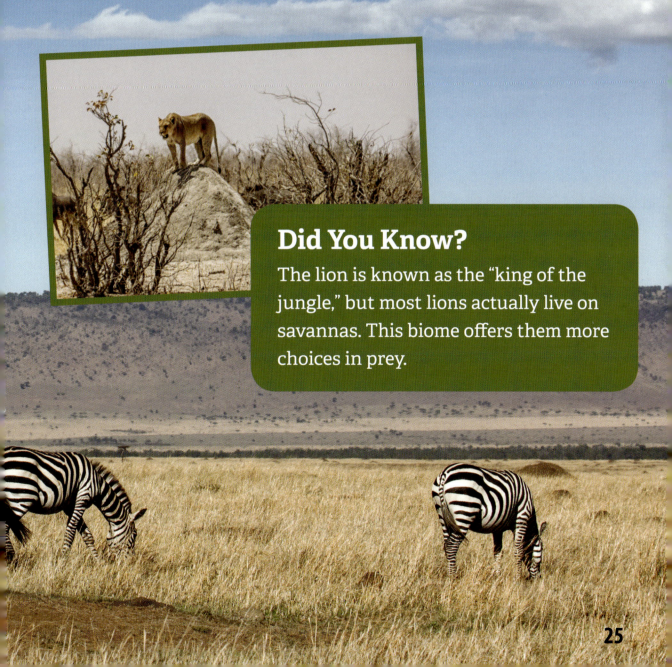

As termites work, they add air to the soil around them. This helps more plants and acacia trees grow near the mound. Baboons, impalas, zebras, and wildebeest gather by mounds to eat fresh grasses. Giraffes come there to eat leaves and the new shoots on acacia trees. Elephants use the mounds as scratching posts. Leopards, cheetahs, and lions perch on top of mounds to look for **prey**.

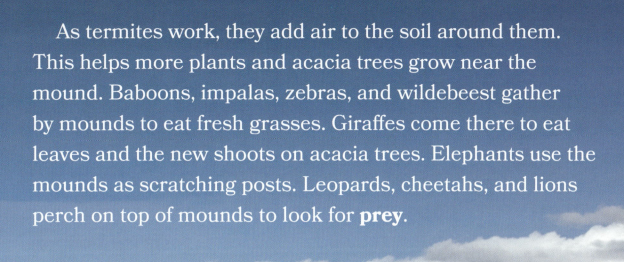

Did You Know?

The lion is known as the "king of the jungle," but most lions actually live on savannas. This biome offers them more choices in prey.

The mounds protect termites from predators, but they still are in danger. Bat-eared foxes, serval cats, mongooses, hyenas, aardvarks, and armadillos all have sharp hearing. They hear termites moving underground. These animals break holes in the mound and suck the termites out.

armadillo

mongoose

aardvark

bat-eared fox

monitor lizard

Even **abandoned** mounds serve the biome. Squirrels, mongooses, and meerkats live in them. Monitor lizards use old mounds as nests for their eggs.

The animals living in grassland biomes depend on the environment and each other to survive. Each animal has adapted physically or socially to the unique conditions of their grassland home.

A female gazelle will hide her babies among tall grasses on the savanna to keep them safe from predators.

ACTIVITY: The Picky Eater Game

The black-footed ferret is one of the most endangered mammals in North America. Prairie dogs are 90 percent of its diet. The amount of land available for prairie dog towns is shrinking. Play this game to see why the loss in prairie dog towns has caused the loss of many black-footed ferrets.

Supplies

65 small squares of colored paper. Label them as follows:
- 5 of each: birds, rabbits, eggs, snakes, mice/rats, lizards, deer, grasses/berries, porcupines, voles, and insects
- 10: prairie dogs

6 sheets of colored paper. Label them as follows:
1. HAWK diet: snakes, rabbits, birds, prairie dogs, mice/rats, lizards
2. BOBCAT diet: rabbits, birds, prairie dogs, mice/rats
3. MOUNTAIN LION diet: deer, rabbits, prairie dogs, grasses/berries, porcupines
4. BADGER diet: voles, mice/rats, prairie dogs, rabbits, lizards, birds, eggs, insects
5. COYOTE diet: voles, rabbits, birds, prairie dogs, mice/rats, snakes, lizards, deer, insects, eggs, grasses/berries
6. BLACK-FOOTED FERRET diet: prairie dogs

1 die

Directions

1. Roll the die.
2. Feed the animal that matches the number you rolled. Place one of the squares that matches something in its diet on the paper.
3. Keep rolling until the ferret runs out of food. How many rolls did the ferret survive? Which animal ran out of food first? Why?

Glossary

abandoned (uh-BAN-duhnd): no longer used for its original purpose

burrows (BUR-ohs): tunnels, holes, or dens dug under the surface of the ground and used as animal homes

decomposers (dee-kuhm-POZE-urs): living things that feed on and break down dead plants and animals

migrate (MYE-grate): to move from one region to another

nocturnal (nahk-TUR-nahl): active at night

nutritious (noo-TRISH-uhs): providing substances needed for good health

prey (pray): an animal that is hunted by another animal for food

savannas (suh-VAN-uhs): flat, grassy plains with few or no trees growing in tropical or subtropical climates

steppes (steps): wide, treeless plains in southeastern Europe or Asia

temperate (TEM-pur-it): having a moderate climate with very few extreme highs or lows in temperature

Index

Text-Dependent Questions

1. What are the main differences between temperate and tropical grasslands?

2. How do prairie chickens survive cold winters on the prairie?

3. How do prairie dogs help other living things in their biome?

4. Why do some animals on the steppes live in herds?

5. Describe three ways other animals use termite mounds.

Extension Activity

Pick the type of grassland biome you think would best support human communities. Make a diagram to show how the natural parts of that biome support each other. Then add in the human community. How will the people, buildings, and human activity affect the natural parts of the biome? Explain your ideas to a friend.

About the Author

Lisa Colozza Cocca has enjoyed reading and learning new things for as long as she can remember. She lives in New Jersey by the coast and loves the feel of the sand between her toes. You can learn more about Lisa and her work at www.lisacolozzacocca.com.

PHOTO CREDITS: Cover and Title Pg ©Nemyrivskyi Viacheslav, ©noreefly, ©KenCanning, ©mzurawski, ©Krisztian Farkas; Pg 28, 31, 32 ©Luseen; Pg 3, 6, 8, 13, 17, 23 ©noreefly; Pg 4 ©CarlaNichiata, Pg 5 ©ttsz; Pg 6 ©tomofbluesprings; Pg 7 ©jaturunp; Pg 8 ©Jillian Cooper; Pg 9 ©mlharing; Pg 10 ©FRANKHILDEBRAND, ©AnjanSapkota; Pg 11 ©photographybyJHWilliams; Pg 12 ©By Brian A Wolf; Pg 13 ©Zoltan Tarlacz; Pg 14 ©Missing35mm; Pg 15 ©By Kerry Hargrove; Pg 16 ©JasonOndreicka; Pg 17 ©Ozbalci; Pg 18 ©Serhii Moiseiev, ©User10095428_393; Pg 19 ©fotohalo; Pg 20 ©powerofforever; Pg 21 ©By karamysh; Pg 22 ©Global_Pics; Pg 23 ©WLDavies; Pg 24 ©GomezDavid, ©Nick Shillan; Pg 25 ©Binty; Pg 26 ©twildlife, ©Shongololo90, ©gregul, ©EcoPic, ©pjmalsbury; Pg 27 ©By Jonathan Oberholster; Pg 28 ©Blair Costelloe

Edited by: Kim Thompson
Cover design by: Kathy Walsh
Interior design by: Rhea Magaro-Wallace

Library of Congress PCN Data

Grassland Animals / Lisa Colozza Cocca
 (Biome Beasts)
  ISBN 978-1-73161-444-5 (hard cover)
  ISBN 978-1-73161-239-7 (soft cover)
  ISBN 978-1-73161-549-7 (e-Book)
  ISBN 978-1-73161-654-8 (ePub)
Library of Congress Control Number: 2019932144

Rourke Educational Media
Printed in the United States of America,
North Mankato, Minnesota